DARK ENERGY TO EUROPE

Russell Bittner

Oh, stop bloviating! That was me IM'ing KeewizzKid half a world and ten hours away. *You haven't even had breakfast yet!* I typed when he didn't immediately answer—then added *LOL* just for giggles. Still nothing. I figured he was probably stuck on 'bloviating.' Guys don't like it when girls use big words they don't know—especially when those girls are non-native-English-speaking girls. KeewizzKid was in Auckland; I was in Paris. It was Friday evening, almost ten o'clock local time—almost eight o'clock in the morning his time. *Saturday* morning, *pour en être précise.*

I'd kept KeewizzKid awake all night with my wit and charm—oh, and with an occasional pix. Nothing too naughty, mind you, but suggestive enough to keep his fingers busy. On the *keyboard,* of course. I didn't want him doing any of that other yucky stuff. Not on *my* time. Or wit. Or charm.

Still no answer. I quickly surfed to M-W.org, typed in the word and pulled up the entry:

bloviate

Main Entry:

blo·vi·ate

Pronunciation:

\blō-vē-āt\

Function:

intransitive verb

Inflected Form(s):

blo·vi·at·ed; **blo·vi·at·ing**

Etymology:

perhaps irregular from [1]*blow*

Date:

circa 1879

: to speak or write verbosely and windily

— **blo·vi·a·tion** \blō-vē-ā-shən\ *noun*

I opened Word, did a copy and paste, attached it to an email and sent all of it winging across two oceans. I hummed the opening bars of *La Marseillaise,* then waited five more seconds; still no answer. I decided he must've finally fallen asleep—guys tend to do that when they suddenly have to think. Maybe he got lost—or at least winded—on 'Etymology.'

Nightie-night! I IM'ed, then added a smiley face before signing off and putting my laptop into hibernation mode. I wasn't yet ready for bed—and felt a bit hungry. These being hard times, I thought I'd just pop into the kitchen to see what Mumsie might've prepared for Sunday lunch. Surely, she wouldn't mind a little preprandial taste test.

I bounded down the stairs, taking two or three at a time. When I turned the corner at the bottom and walked into the kitchen, *papa* was sitting at the table—a wineglass in one hand, a journal of some sort or other in the other. He immediately put both down; stood up; then went to fetch a second wineglass, which I knew was for me. That's the kind of dad he is.

"Comment ça va, chérie?" he asked in transit to a small room just off the kitchen—our *cave*—where he stored his wine and wineglasses. Our *cave* was just large enough for two people, sitting *tête-à-tête,* to get cozy while discussing esoteric love—or lovelorn esoterica. Whenever *papa* or *maman* announced to me or to Robert—my younger brother—that they were going off to the *cave* to discuss 'affairs of state,' we knew better. My mother was a professor of anthropology; my father, of astrophysics. But neither was sufficiently adequate to draw them into the *cave* for a little *tête-à-tête*—and so, Robert and I would smartly remain upstairs, in our rooms, until the state had been put right once again.

"Jamais meilleure, papa! Jamais meilleure." It was something I'd once heard in an American film, and I actually preferred it in English: "never better."

"Jamais mieux, mon petit cru. 'Meilleur' est un adjectif. 'Mieux,' un adverbe. Ne confonds pas les deux. Tu y es, mon son et lumière?"

"D'accord, mon raisin-d'être. J'y suis." Papa was a scientist, but he was also French. And a Frenchman—*every* Frenchman—is first and foremost a guardian of the language. At the same time, and because he was a Frenchman, he was a fool for endearments—and for puns. *Mon petit* or *premier cru* was one such—as was *mon son et lumière.* Calling me his *petit choux* would've been just too plebian. This, of course, was my reason for calling *him* my 'grapeful being.' I am, after all, my father's daughter.

As I opened the fridge, I peeked over at his journal and saw that it had an English-language title.

"Américain ou anglais?" I asked.

"Ni l'un, ni l'autre," he said. *"Des Indes."*

"Boeuf!" I said apropos of nothing. I looked more carefully at the cover: ***Journal of Astrophysics and Astronomy***, *a quarterly journal in English, published by the Indian Academy of Sciences.*

Papa poured me a glass of wine as I set down a bowl and soup spoon, then helped myself to some of *maman*'s vichyssoise. He raised his glass to mine for a toast—then immediately forgot his original intent as he paused to inspect the contents of his glass.

"Chambolle-Musigny," he said. *"Une excellente année."*

"Oui, papa," I said as I took a sip and let the wine sit for a moment on my tongue as he'd once taught me to do.

"À la tienne," I said with what I hoped—because I *meant* it—was a genuine show of gratitude for his ushering me, his seventeen-year-old daughter, through this little door into the world of adult pleasures.

He put his glass down, and I noted how his eyebrows arched together as he reached for a cigarette. They looked like the folds of a curtain pulled back to reveal a stage. He was preparing himself—and me, too—for drama.

"Marie-Claire, ta mère et moi nous sommes décidés à t'envoyer à faire un stage à l'étranger."

I stared at him *bouche bée*—then tentatively reached for one of his cigarettes. His glance at my hand as I extended it in the direction of his pack let me know in no uncertain terms there was a limit to adult pleasures I could count on in his company.

"S'il te plaît, Marie-Claire." It was not an invitation.

"Oui, papa," I said as I withdrew my hand.

He lit his cigarette, exhaled, reached up to his lip to remove a stray bit of tobacco, and resumed. *En plus, nous nous sommes décidés pour les États-Unis. Alors, dorénavant il ne nous faut causer, deviser, bavarder même qu'en anglais—afin d'améliorer tes connaissances. J'espère bien que tu en puisses comprendre—."*

"Comment, papa?"

"No, my child. From this moment on, only in English. We have to ameliorate your knowledges."

"*Mais, papa!*" I whined in my best imito-American.

"*Non!* Not another locution from you that is not in English—or rather, in American English."

I was already way ahead of him. *Mon pauvre, petit papa,* stuck in his silly Gallic ways, he couldn't even hear it. Every centimeter—no, every *inch,* I quickly corrected myself—the French professor of astrophysics that he was. Sunk in his books when he wasn't lecturing—lecturing me, that is, or my younger brother. Or at least one of his students, all of whom hung on his every word like puppies on a bitch's teats. Or debating—always debating—with his English and American colleagues: black holes;

string theory; the cosmological constant; universe versus the multiverse.

But as much as I loved him (and he *me*—never did I doubt it), I realized he was an antique, a fuddy-duddy, a warrior of the old school still trying to fight in neat ranks against guerillas. *Moi?* I'd figured out years earlier there was only one way to defeat the enemy, and that was with the enemy's own weapons. With those knowledges (oh, my too, dear *papa!*), I watched British and American television, studied the idiom, the inflexions, even the facial contortions—then perfected all of it in real-time on the Web.

The Web was *their* Maginot Line. It was obvious to me and to *mes copains* that the Brits, the Yanks, the Aussies and the Kiwis thought they controlled it. And indeed, for any number of years, they had—at least the Americans. They'd owned the content, the meta-language, the icons, the woof and the warp of the Web. But we French, *alors,* we're not stupid. Sure, we had our *Indochine;* but we got out! The Americans poured in—they thought they knew better. Well, they *didn't.* Just as they don't know any better now in Iraq. And if we thought after the first world war—and particularly following WWII—that they were something special, well, we've learned in the meantime they're not.

Instead, we're looking east to learn what the Chinese have known for centuries—known even before we Europeans knew it—and we're discovering the wisdom of their older ways. For instance, how to fight using your enemy's strengths in things like jujutsu, kung fu and Muay Thai. There's not really much we have here in France…Renault? Citroën? Dom Pérignon? The Eiffel Tower? But we have brains. And with our brains, we can work magic.

Oh, and *charm.* We have that—as the Americans like to say—*in spades!*

Speaking of which, and in exchange for sharing just a *soupçon* of my French charm with him one summer in *Basse-Normandie*, an American acquaintance once lent me a copy of P. J. O'Rourke's "Unwanted Foreigners." It was an amusing treatise, to say the least, but I believe O'Rourke got at least one of his facts wrong. He writes in his essay that the French invented the blow-job. But I think the real credit for that belongs to the Italians. Yes, they erected it—even if we French perfected it.

Anyway, *papa, maman,* Robert and I had taken a day trip to Mont-Saint-Michel, where I met this young American. I knew the tides; he didn't. He gave me the essay. I suggested he walk out onto the beach while I read it. The ocean came rushing in—and poof! One less American. Instead, one more little book for my library.

"*Papa?*"

"No, my child. You must say 'Father'—or 'Dad.' Just please not to say 'Daddy'—for both our sakes."

"Father—," I said obediently.

"Yes, my child?"

"Father, where would you have me go in those United States?"

"In those United States," he said, "I would have you go to the California. Your mother and I have already arranged for you to stay with Professor Perlmutter and his wife, whom you once meeted here in Paris two years ago when they assisted at the Conference on the Joint Dark Energy Mission. You may recall to yourself we invited them out to our place in Lower Normandy for the weekend following the conference."

"I meeted them, Father? *Ouf!* I don't recall to myself at *all!*" (I thought it bad form to correct the professor's English. You don't play to an adversary's weaknesses; you play to his *strengths.)*

"You did indeed, my darling daughter, and you will again. We have secured transport for you, and you shall leave here at the end of next week to spend the entire month of August with the family Perlmutter in California. This is a family of much esteem, by the way, as *both* Monsieur and Madame Perlmutter are established professors."

"But I will miss you and Mummy so, Father!"

"They don't say 'Mummy' in those United States, *mon petit cru*. They say 'Mom.' You may say 'Mom' or 'Mother.' Just please not to say 'Mommy' or 'Mummy.'"

"I will miss *both* my mother and my father—but especially my father!" I inserted quite deliberately, as I knew that m*aman* was out of earshot and that *papa* would no doubt have the last word on my cache of spending money.

"And we will miss you, my darling daughter. We will miss you, too," he said as he put his hand up to touch my cheek. "But all birds must leaf the nest—even if just for a short flight to test their wings. If we never leaf, we never learn."

"Yes, father. I know. Leafing is something every bird must do—before, little by little, she can begin to build her own nest."

This much-beloved father of mine, this professor of astrophysics and an all-around polymath, paused with his hand and cigarette *en mi-route* to his mouth and looked at me. 'Perplexed' would be too bland a word to describe his expression of bemusement, and I was suddenly overcome with shame. My love of French proverbs and punditry was still stronger than my budding appreciation of the wisdom of the Orient. I needed discipline. "The California"—I decided in that instant—would be good for me. It would force me to spend long hours on the beach in contemplation of ephemera.

The following week came and went in a flurry of preparations. *Maman* gave me money to buy myself some new clothes, and I spent most of it on bikinis. After all, I reasoned, bikinis were the only suitable wardrobe for the study of wave theory. What? Would she have me dressing up like Marie Curie? *Ouf!* To complete my wardrobe and demonstrate—at least ostensibly—that *maman*'s money had been well spent, I visited a thrift shop and bought enough *bric-à-brac* to fill up two suitcases. I knew she'd never look. That was the kind of mother she was.

The night before my scheduled departure, *maman* made an unusual trip to my bedroom, where both suitcases stood ready and waiting for inspection if she chose to do so. She first knocked—as she always does—and awaited my permission to enter.

"*Entrée libre et gratuite,*" I said, not knowing—but suspecting—who might be rapping at my chamber door. (I'd just been re-reading Poe in the original in preparation for my descent into California darkness.)

"*C'est moi, cherie,*" *maman* said as she pushed the door open and stepped inside. *Maman's* terms of endearment tended towards the mundane. It was everything *else* she said that bordered on the celestial. "*Tout prête?*" she asked.

"I am, mother. Quite ready." I was bound and determined—especially now when I feared *maman* might be ready to embark on a sentimental journey—to keep *papa*'s "Only English Spoken Here" diktat in full force. I knew that *maman*'s English was in fact considerably more studied than *papa*'s, but I thought that if we now confronted each other like two strangers in a strange land, there'd be less risk of exchanges from the heart. I wanted no sappiness on this, the eve of my voyage to the New World.

"Then perhaps we can talk a bit," she said. "There's something of which I need to make you aware."

"Please, mother, fire away!" *Maman* had never shown herself to be reticent on any topic—sex, drugs, rock 'n' roll, the smell of anchovies or Roquefort cheese—with either Robert or me from the moment we were old and curious enough to ask questions. She'd also never bored either of us with philosophical discussions unless we'd specifically asked—and even then, her method was always Socratic. Can one ask for a better *maman*? *Je pense pas.*

"Let me be brief and to the point," she said—as she always was. "Americans are a bit funny about body hair." She paused to see how I might react. I realized this was my cue to register surprise.

"Really?" I said. "About body hair—but not about head hair. *Ouf!"*

"Yes, it's true. They're a bit funny about hygiene in general, but particularly about body hair."

"Oh, you mean they *bathe* a lot. Yes, I read that somewhere." I knew that if I pretended to be entirely ignorant of this culture I was about to conquer, *maman* might get suspicious—or worse, solicitous. The last thing I needed, on the eve of my venture into the New World, was a solicitous *maman.*

"Well, they actually shower more than they bathe. Bathing is too time-consuming for them—that, or too sensual. They're afraid of what crimes of passion they might commit after forty-five minutes in a bathtub."

We exchanged smiles. I liked that *maman* would share her adult humor with me.

"No, only daughter of mine, their real"—and here she stumbled with the pronunciation of a word even *I* had problems with—"pecul-, peculiarity lies in the matter of body hair. They shave their—" and at this point, she gestured towards her armpit (not, I was certain, because she couldn't or wouldn't pronounce the word, but because she might not know it). *Maman* was no Puritan, but 'armpit' was simply a word she wouldn't have bothered to commit to memory.

"*Dis donc,*" I said. "*Ils se rasent les aisselles.*"

"*Elles,*" she corrected. "The *women* shave themselves in that place."

"Ouf!" I said. "*Quelle bizarrerie!*"

Maman suddenly laughed her best manic laugh, and I realized why I loved her to distraction. I also realized, however, that I was off the hook; that she'd thought she was delivering a real bit of news to me; that I'd convinced her I was too young, or too innocent, or too unschooled in the ways of the world to know that some women outside of France shave their armpits. I decided this was *not* a good moment to educate *maman* on the benefits of a three-quarter Brazilian, the cut of which I'd known for the better part of two years.

"Well, she said as she wiped her eyes, "I am glad we had this little chat. I am certain that if you have any other questions or confusions about life in the United States, Dr. Nelson—that's Laura Nelson, the wife of Dr. Perlmutter—will be only too happy and sufficiently well-endowed to answer them. She is a professor of anthropology."

"Of anthropology, *maman?* *Papa* said of astrophysics." 'Endowed' and 'equipped' were easily confused, even in French. I decided that discretion was the better part of ardor—and a very real filial ardor was what I felt for my mother at that moment.

"I shall now leave you to your packing, *mon petit faon*. We shall be leaving tomorrow morning promptly at eight for *Orly. Bonne nuit.* Goodnight," she added in English as she left my room and closed the door upon exiting.

Merde! I thought to myself. I could feel my eyes welling up—the last thing I needed on the eve of my discovery of the New World. She'd called me her 'little fawn' ever since I was a baby. It had had no effect on me all of my growing-up years—until quite recently, that is. Now, perhaps because she saved it only for special occasions, I'd get teary-eyed whenever she said it—and so, thankfully, she said it rarely.

I decided I needed an antidote—and that the best and easiest cure would be a quick visit to say *mes adieux* to my brother, Robert. I walked down the hall and knocked on his bedroom door—now sealed off to, and from, all human traffic except for those instances, at regular intervals, when an obnoxious mouth—namely his own—came out to fill his stomach, or the other end came out just as noxiously to empty it.

"*Qui vive?*" he shouted. Robert had made of his bedroom a fortress with the idea of defending *la France.* He wasn't yet old enough to know about Waterloo.

"*C'est moi,*" I sighed. *Papa*'s diktat did not extend to Robert—who spoke only in French, thought only in French, ate, shat and pissed only in French. An English word out of his mouth would've been an abomination, and my ears—just to name a pair—would've preferred the feel of boiling oil poured from a cauldron.

"*Entre s'il faut,*" he said.

I pushed the door open—slowly, so as not to frighten off any wolves he might now be feeding under his bed. "*Et alors,* I said as I saw him lying on the floor, flipping through some trashy bit of anime. "*Comment est-ce que tu vas passer ces quatre semaines de mon effroyable absence?*" I asked. I didn't really care how he was going to spend August. But in the spirit of sisterly love, I inquired.

He dropped the magazine slowly to the floor, let a stupid grin grow upon his face, raised his arm to just above his crotch, and began to make an obscene up and down motion with a closed fist. So much, I thought, for the spirit of *brotherly* love.

"*Mais comme tu es dégueulasse!*" I said. Whatever had welled up in my eyes just moments earlier disappeared as in the air of Gobi. "*Alors, on se verra en septembre, mon petit bonbombe.*" It was my own particular choice of endearment for a brother who was neither choice nor dear. I closed his door and went back to my room.

July had been unusually pleasant—even for Paris. A breeze now blew through my bedroom window, and on it rode the prayerful song of church bells in a paean to midnight. I didn't know whether I'd find church bells in the New World. I didn't know whether I'd find breezes even—though I was relatively certain France was not alone in having weather or wind. Yes, I was French—and hardly ashamed of my Frenchiosity. But on this, the eve of my conquest of the New World, I was also of an open mind. Things could be different, and that wouldn't necessarily be bad. Things could look, taste, smell and feel different, but I wouldn't dismiss them out of hand because one or more of their aspects might be unfamiliar to me. A behavior might be barbarous—which is to say, not French—but I would judge it on its own merits. We French have no monopoly on decorum, on wit, on civilization. We have a monopoly only on *French* decorum, *French* wit and *French* civilization. Oh, and on charm. *That* monopoly we have in spades.

Perhaps now is a good time, dearest reader, to declare another special occasion for clarification and to reveal to you that this is as much a memoir as a story. I'm no longer an adolescent girl living In

Paris. Where I live and what I do for a living are both items I will reveal to you at an appropriate time later in this memoir. But for the moment, suffice it to say -- if I may be so bold -- that I am considerably older and wiser than the time and place I chose to open this memoir with. And so, let's hurry on back to the olde world and to gay Paree.

The next morning, I didn't need an alarm to wake me up. The sun rises early over Paris in July and August, and it rose—or so it seemed to me—especially early that morning on *my* account. The first day of August was going to be a hot one in Paris—hot most of all for the thousands of Parisians locked up in their cars and heading down to the Midi for the start of their summer holidays. Me, I was headed someplace else. How hot it would be there was still a mystery to me. I could've easily looked it up on the Web, but I wanted this mystery to remain just that until I actually set foot in my New World.

I put on a summer dress—nothing too frilly, yet just fanciful and frivolous enough to excite interest in my fellow passengers should any of them turn out to be of the right age and disposition. Spaniards have a little proverb I quite like: "*No es la ropa sino la percha.*" ("It's not the clothes, but the hanger.") A rather petulant young man from Madrid—as he liked to call himself, a *chulo madrileño*—taught it to me one summer in exchange for a *soupçon* of French charm. He was obviously trying to tell me something, but I pretended not to understand. After all, there weren't a lot of clothes on my particular 'hanger' at the time, and he seemed intent on relieving me of the few that still remained. As he was clearly much too full of himself for my liking, I dispatched him with a French *coup de grâce.*

I blew Robert—still fast asleep—a begrudging kiss through his bedroom door as I brought my suitcases downstairs and out to the car. *Maman* and *papa* were finishing up their coffee and croissants in the kitchen when I came back inside.

"Good morning, Mother. Good morning, Father," I said as I gave each of them, in turn, a kiss on both cheeks.

"Marie-Claire, you should finally know that Americans do not give each other such kisses," my father instructed me.

"Americans do not much kiss at all," my mother added, "unless it is of a sexual nature. Then they call it 'French kissing.'"

"French kissing, *maman?*" I said.

"*Oui, cherie.* It is out of their puritanical guilt that they attribute such a kiss to us."

"But what is 'French kissing?' I asked again—as if I'd already forgotten the Italian boy with whom I'd shared a funicular in Val-d'Isère the previous winter. In exchange for a tad more than a *soupçon* of my French charm, he'd shown me some Italian tongue. Funny, he didn't call it 'French kissing' at the time. He just did it, and I did it back. Which is why, for months thereafter, I used to think of it as my 'Alpine kiss.' He *schussed* into my mouth, and I *schussed* into his for the twenty-three-minute length of the ride up to the Col de L'Iseran.

"We shall talk about that on our way to the airport," *maman* said.

"Yes," *papa* said. "We should get a move in."

And a move *in* is what we got. I checked myself and my bags at the counter, and *papa* got permission for himself and *maman* to accompany me to the gate—where we chatted in English and waited patiently for my boarding call. *Papa* showed me a picture of my hosts-to-be and gave me a couple of bottles of his best bourgogne, wrapped and beribboned, to present to my hosts. He must've reminded me half a dozen times that Professor Perlmutter's name was 'Saul'—but that I was not to call him that unless and until he invited me to do so—that his wife's name was 'Laura Nelson,' and that their little girl's name was 'Noa.' I asked *papa* whether Noa was also an astrophysicist, just like her *maman* and *papa*.

"Oh, no, my darling daughter. She is still just a little bean of a thing," he said. "But soon, no doubt, she will become one," he added—and I saw *maman* roll her eyes.

When my boarding call finally came, I surprised even myself. "*Merde!*" I said under my breath in an effort to vulgarize the pathos of the moment.

And yet, when I think back to that moment, I realize—now as then—that a woman, even an adult woman, is and will always remain her parents' little girl. It was when I reached up to hug them both farewell; when I felt a warm wetness on my cheek that I knew had not come from my own eyes; when I looked into theirs and saw its source; it was then that something like the proverbial walnut leapt up into my throat. Suddenly, *my* eyes were gushing—from what cause, I'm still not sure even today. But of one thing I'm quite certain: it wasn't shame. Never had I felt ashamed to feel the love—and several years later, the loss—of my parents. At that moment, as we stood hugging and weeping into each other's arms, we needed no words, either in French or in English, to convey to each other the singular fondness that each of us felt, one for the other.

Today, more often than not, I see unhappy families. And although I think I understand the source of their unhappiness, the gift of my birth family is one that cannot be shared. I cannot replace ill-equipped parents with my parents, or even set mine up as an example—for mine are dead. They live on only through me, now married to a man who is more like my father than any other man I've ever met. It's no accident that we are attracted to—and may eventually marry—someone just like our opposite sex parent. This is something I, as a psychologist, am now quite certain of.

But I digress—unlike my mother; and lecture—just like my father. I have a story yet to tell … of a voyage to, and a conquest of, the New World.

Once I was seated and belted in, I put on my earphones. As my seat was on the starboard side of the jet, our take-off in a westerly direction allowed me a perfect view of the *Île de la Cité* and of *Notre Dame de Paris*—then, split seconds later, of the *Tour Eiffel* and the *Arc de Triomphe*. Pride in France's national monuments was not something I particularly felt; yet I suspected, at that moment, I might miss the sights I'd otherwise taken for granted in my everyday ocular life. No matter: I knew I'd have the Golden Gate Bridge to gaze at in just under twelve hours.

And just under twelve hours later, that's exactly what I had. I'd apparently fallen asleep as soon as we'd left Paris—and then slept the entire way over. My earphones had kept out any extraneous sounds, and the flight attendants, I suspected, had decided I needed sleep more than food. As we began our descent into San Francisco, I felt thoroughly rested—even if a bit cramped.

To work out my muscle cramps, I decided to walk up and down the aisle a couple of times while I made a quick calculation. We'd been in the air for almost twelve hours, but this fact was superfluous—one of those bits of data that get inserted into a math problem to try to confuse you. I knew that the time difference between Paris and San Francisco was nine hours. And so, if it was now ten o'clock at night in Paris I noted as I looked at my watch, the local time would be one o'clock in the afternoon.

Moments later, the captain came over the public address system to welcome us to San Francisco—and to announce the local time. *Ouf!*

As I exited the plane, I started to look immediately for my hosts. That's when I saw—and instantly recognized— *la famille* Perlmutter.

I walked directly up to them, stretched out my hand in imitation of the American girls I'd seen make such a gesture on YouTube or shows like "American Idol," "Fear Factor" and "The Weakest Link," and introduced myself with a big, toothy smile and the best Southern accent I could conjure up.

"Howdy y'all! My name's Louisiana Purchase."

"Well, well," Dr. Nelson said with a grin. "If she ain't a chip off the old block."

"A *chip* off the old block!" Noa repeated.

"Just that!" I said as I crouched down and put my hand out to shake the hand of a little girl who looked neither like her mother nor like her father, but rather like something out of the future. She didn't hesitate, but took it in hers and gave it a toddler's pump as she looked me straight in the eye. I decided at that instant that I shouldn't underestimate Americans' claim to the future, or overestimate the power of *French* charm.

"Welcome to America," Dr. Nelson said.

"Yes, indeed," added Dr. Perlmutter, "and to San Francisco."

"I thank you both, Professor Nelson and Professor Perlmutter" I said as I put my hand out to shake first her hand and then his. She instead grasped me lightly by the shoulders and planted a kiss on both my cheeks.

"And please call me 'Laura,' she said.

Professor Perlmutter awaited his turn, then repeated the greeting. "And please call me 'Saul.'

I next looked at their little girl in her stroller and crouched down to meet her at eye level. She'd clearly been observing our adult ceremony with keen interest. "*Both* cheeks, please," she said as she pointed first to one dimple and then to the other. "And please call me 'Noa,'" she said with what I swear was a *soupçon* of irony. How a four-year-old—even a *French* four-year-old—could demonstrate irony was beyond me. But I didn't doubt it in Noa's case even for an instant.

On the ride from the airport to their home in Sausalito, we stopped off at Half Moon Bay for my first taste of a smoothie. It wasn't as sugary sweet as I'd come to believe all American food was; rather, it was fruity sweet. *We could learn a thing or two from these Americans,* I thought.

As I sipped my smoothie and took my first view of the Pacific, Saul turned north and then drove us through San Francisco on our way to the Golden Gate Bridge. I took in an occasional site, but was much more interested in the little girl sitting next to me in the back seat. Her parents chose graciously not to interrupt our play except once to point out Golden Gate Park, and then again to point out the bridge as we were actually approaching it via the Presidio.

"It's a shame, Marie-Claire, that your first view of the Golden Gate won't be at sunset," Laura said. "But something tells me you'll have other opportunities before you leave us."

"I'm sure I will, too," I said—letting my brief answer suffice as I turned my full attention to the bridge and to San Francisco Bay beneath it. We had no equivalent in Paris, and I understood for perhaps the first time in my life that we French had no monopoly either on engineering genius or on architectural majesty. Although I suspect both Saul and Laura understood quite well that they lived in a beautiful city, they clearly had no need to flaunt it.

As a result, I took it all in at my own pace, in my own way, and at my own rate of appreciation. I was already beginning to think this might be one *other* quite exceptional family.

When we finally arrived at their front door, I was immensely pleased to see that it was located directly across from a small park, the name of which I was to learn only the next day. It suited their style, their temperament—and no doubt, their pocketbook. Nothing too formal, showy or ostentatious; just an informal place of green, shade and benches. From the little I'd seen of the neighborhood once we'd gotten off the bridge, it, too, seemed like a comfortable place—neither urban nor suburban. Just somehow appropriate—and very much what I'd expected California to be.

Saul took my bags, and Noa took my hand—and Laura took the lead and opened the front door for all of us. "Noa, would you please show Marie-Claire to her room?" Laura asked, then turned to me. "If you'd like to take a bath or a shower—or perhaps a nap—please feel free. Saul and I have both taken the afternoon off, so we'll just be putzing around the garden if we're not in the library or in the kitchen."

I made a mental note to look up this word 'putzing' just as soon as I could get my laptop set up. I thought I had a pretty good handle on the English language—but, as both *maman* and *papa* never tired of reminding me, *'Une langue, c'est un océan dont on ne connaît que les bords.'*

Acculturation is not a pec-u-liar-ly (*Ouf!* I had as much trouble thinking the word as *maman* had saying it) French talent or skill—yet in wanting not to offend my guests, I decided to accept Laura's invitation. "A shower would be lovely," I said. "But I'm not in the least bit tired or sleepy. I'll come down and join you in the garden just as soon as I've had a chance to freshen up."

Laura smiled, and Noa walked me slowly up the stairs. For a four-year-old, they were big stairs—but she took them carefully and seemed to be more concerned about *my* ability to do the same. Perhaps, I thought, she sees me as a middling creature—or, with my strange accent, as a Middle Earth creature—and wonders whether there are stairs in whatever part of Middle Earth I come from.

"Wanna see my room first?" she asked—and I knew in that instant that *she* knew we were both just girls at heart.

"I'd *love* to!" I said—at which point, Noa beamed.

She began the tour as soon as we entered her room, pointing out first one item and then the other. "This is my bed," she said, "and this is my play area. Here is my closet and here is my dresser—." As she continued her commentary on the obvious, I was struck by the room's austerity. I'd naturally expected—as much from T.V. shows and movies I'd seen as from anything I'd picked up on the Web—that an American child's bedroom would be chockablock full of toys and games and God-knows-what other paraphernalia. Hers was not. It was positively Spartan. There were no little bears on her bed sheets, no stuffed animals on her pillow. There was a half-crazed-looking marionette hanging *over* her bed, but nothing else on the walls or floor.

I walked with her over to her play area and was further astounded when she showed me a box filled with popsicle sticks, wine corks, bottle tops and other assorted throw-away items that could've come from most any kitchen. And yet, not only did she show them to me with a quiet kind of pride, she then put the box back on the shelf in its rightful place.

"I also have a library," she said—and indeed she did. I looked at the titles on the spines of a couple of dozen large picture-books: *Complete Fairy Tales* by the Brothers Grimm; *Selected Fairytales* by H. C. Andersen; *Pinocchio* by Collodi; *The Classic Mother Goose; The Æsop for Children;* and a collection of three books— *Amphigorey, Amphigorey Too,* and *Amphigorey Also*—by an author I'd never heard of before: Edward Gorey. What I next saw absolutely flabbergasted me: *The Complete Fables* of Jean de La Fontaine—not to mention the same *père et fils* de Brunhoff *Babar* series and Ludwig Bemelman's *Madeline* series I'd grown up with. I reached down and pulled one of the *Babar* books off the shelf. The illustrations were identical, but the text was obviously in English.

And that's when I hit upon my little August project.

"Noa," I said. "How would you like to learn a bit of French this month?"

Her eyes grew large and round—just like her mouth until it was defeated by a sharp intake of breath. Then, she waved her arms, and it became clear to me once again that I was speaking with an excited little toddler and not with a world-weary child prodigy.

"Oh, yes!" she said. "Yes, yes, *yes!*"

I held out my hand to shake on the deal. "*Soit!*" I said with a smile.

"*Soit!*" she said in turn as she held out her own hand. She obviously had no idea what the word meant, but the context was apparently sufficient. We'd just completed our first French lesson—and the exercise in deal-making was a little value-added.

I took a shower and wrapped myself in a pair of towels, called *maman* and *papa* to let them know I'd arrived safely, then lay down for what I thought would be a couple of minutes to rest my eyes. When I next opened them, it was Saturday morning. Little hands were on my face, and tiny fingers were pushing up my eyelids. “Wake up, wake up!” Noa whispered delicately into my ear. Her fingers, however, were less courteous.

I pushed her hand away and covered my head with a pillow until, seconds later, I became conscious enough to realize this was not Robert pulling one of his pranks, and I was no longer in Paris—at which point, I sat straight up in bed. Noa was pouting and seemingly on the verge of tears until I reached over the side of the bed, picked her up and stuffed her in next to me. I was sleeping *au naturel*—as Anglophones are quite fond of saying—and Noa appeared to find my state of dishabille a source of fascination and merriment. She immediately threw back the covers and began exploring. Was she perhaps thinking that French and American girls had different anatomies? I wasn’t by nature, disposition or education, shy. At the same time, I didn’t know what an American mother and father might think appropriate or inappropriate for a child of Noa’s age and curiosity.

“Why don’t we go down to breakfast?” I asked, deflection being the better part of valor.

“*Soit!*” she said, which confirmed for me that I had a smart one—but also that we were going to have to find a means to enrich her vocabulary.

Noa insisted upon picking out my wardrobe, and I let her have her way. She found me a pair of jeans and a blouse, but then discovered—and quickly became fascinated by—my underwear. *Surely, she's seen her mother's stock of bras and panties,* I thought. But then, the fascination I saw in her face suggested to me why French lingerie has the reputation it has. Maybe we *do* have something besides Renault, Citroën, Dom Pérignon and the Eiffel Tower.

"Not like Mommy's," she said as she held up a pair of panties. "Not like Mommy's, too," she added as she passed me a bra. She made the same pronouncement a third time as she carefully watched me put it on, but it wasn't the bra she was looking at when she made her pronouncement. I believe I blushed—though I was at least happy she'd chosen not to comment on the three-quarter cut of my Brazilian.

Once I was fully dressed and had—with Noa's help—brushed my hair, she took me again by the hand and walked me downstairs—though not before she'd cautioned me at the top to take them only one at a time. And "carefully," she'd added with a shake of her finger. "You don't wanna do a Vonnegut."

I had *no* idea what she meant.

Laura and Saul were just then sitting down to breakfast in the garden when Noa and I arrived. They met me with a smile and a kiss to both cheeks, which gave me pause to wonder whether I really had recently crossed the Atlantic—until I saw the breakfast spread, that is. My stomach was accustomed, at most, to coffee and a croissant or yogurt at that hour of the day, and I was afraid I might prove to be a rather ungracious guest on my very first day in America.

"There's no obligation," Laura said when she saw my look of consternation. "Eat as much or as little as you like."

"Or even less," Saul said. "Less for you is more for me," he added with a chuckle.

Over breakfast, we discussed the little project I had in mind for Noa. They were absolutely ecstatic about the idea—as if it had never occurred to them that I might be both willing and able to give something back in return for their hospitality. The only problem was, I obviously hadn't brought any of the French-language *Babar* series with me.

"Why don't both of you walk down to the public library after breakfast and see what you can find," Saul suggested.

"Yes," Laura said. "Good idea. I'm quite certain they have at least a piddling foreign-language section at the library. If not, we can order something through Habitat Books."

"Can I come, Mommy?"

"Of course you can, nugget."

Although I didn't know what either 'piddling' or 'nugget' meant, I gathered from the context that the first was somewhat pejorative; the second, a term of endearment. Now I had, with 'putzing,' three new words to look up—and if their meanings weren't *too* dear, a new sobriquet or two I might be able to apply to Robert in the future.

After a leisurely breakfast under a fog-enshrouded California sun, Laura, Noa and I walked down to the local library. The librarian who assisted us was quite friendly—especially after she'd learned I was French and had then decided to try out a few of her book-learned French phrases on me. Most of what she said sounded like something out of the previous century, but I didn't mind. In fact, I was enchanted.

The library did in fact have three volumes in French from Jean de Brunhoff's collection, and two from his son—Laurent's—collection. The remaining volumes of *père et fils* Brunhoff were in English. I selected the *Histoire de Babar, Le Voyage de Babar,* and *Le Roi Babar,* all of which the librarian gave me—or rather, gave to Laura—without hesitation. To me, she gave a "*je vous en prie*" and a curtsy in answer to my "*Merci beaucoup, Madame!*"

On the way back from the library, books in one hand and Noa's five outstretched fingers in the other, I suggested that the three of us stop off at the park directly across from their house. That's when I learned its name: Tiffany Park. *What a delight!* I thought. *So like the lamps I've seen on many occasions.* The park, I could see at a glance, was as much a source of pleasure for children as it was for adults—even if for entirely different reasons. I watched as a number of children went helter-skelter running, skipping, climbing—and I learned another new English-language expression from Laura: monkey bars. I thought … what an appropriate—and then thought maybe I should bring a set back to Robert.

Over lunch—again in the garden—Laura and Saul asked me how I wanted to spend my first Saturday afternoon in America. I thought momentarily about my suitcase full of bikinis and about the sand and waves I'd seen at Half Moon Bay—and then suggested I'd like to spend it with Noa in the park. They looked quizzically first at each other, then at me.

"Marie-Claire," Saul said, "this is your vacation. We didn't bring you here as an *au pair.*"

"Yes, Marie-Claire," Laura then said. "It's very kind of you to offer, but we know that girls of your age have more interesting things to do than to mind young children. Would you like Saul to drive you into the city—perhaps to Golden Gate Park if you have any particular interest in parks?"

"I'd be delighted," Saul quickly offered. "Just say the word."

I could sense that Noa was looking up at me with those same big, round eyes—hoping, and yet steeling herself—for the disappointment of rejection. At the same time, she inched herself around the table and under her mother's arm—perhaps in preparation for this first little abandonment.

"No," I said. "I'd much rather spend the afternoon with Noa."

No sooner were the words out of my mouth than Noa squirted out from under her mother's arm and slipped in under mine. Before either of her parents could once again protest, she held out her little hand to seal the deal. "*Soit!*" she said—and so it was.

"*Nom de Dieu!*" Saul said—and he said it so easily and with such perfect inflection and nasal intonation, I found myself wondering what little secret he and Laura might be keeping from me.

But I was not to be given the opportunity or time to investigate. Instead, Noa took me by the hand and pulled me out of my seat, then led me out the front door and across the street into the park—where she made straight for the monkey bars while I found a watchful position from below. She scrambled up, over and around them with the ease, I thought, of a much older child. But I was beginning to suspect my first real surprise would come only when I learned there might be something she *couldn't* do.

We'd been at the park for perhaps half an hour when I saw a young man who looked to be about my age—or maybe a year or two older—enter accompanied by a little boy. The two of them seemed to be on our very same mission, as the little boy headed directly over to where I was standing and mounted the bars with a single bound. The young man smiled and nodded at me, then turned his full attention to the toddler in his charge.

Either this young man was very good at pretending not to be interested in me, or he simply wasn't—interested, that is. As I couldn't recall this ever having happened to me, I thought he might be *pédé.* In any case, I thought him to be one of the best-looking *mecs* I'd ever seen in my life. He had wavy brown hair, a straight nose, full lips and deep-set, dark eyes. I judged him to be almost two meters tall—very svelte, but certainly not lacking in muscle tone if his forearms were any indication. He was wearing a long-sleeved shirt with the sleeves rolled up and—I demurely dropped my eyes to verify—no wedding band. *This, then, is likely not his child,* I thought. *But if not, what's he doing here on a sunny Saturday afternoon with a toddler? Why isn't he at the beach looking at bikinis? He's clearly pédé,* I decided.

As I turned my full attention back to Noa, I must confess I felt a little foolish. After all, not *every* man had to go gaga the moment he set eyes on me. Most did, but that was beside the point. "Noa, please be careful," I said—though not really knowing why I'd said it, as Noa was not doing anything more dangerous than she'd done the instant before or would do an instant hence. At the same time, I could see that she was fully absorbed in a conversation she was having with the young boy who'd just ascended the bars—and seemed to be offering him words of encouragement to climb to the top, where she now reigned.

"You're French," I suddenly heard from off to the side of me. I looked at him, but didn't immediately answer. "Or Canadian—French Canadian?" he said with one eyebrow raised.

I felt a flutter in my stomach. "Or maybe Belgian," I said through a smirk.

"Or maybe Swiss," he said. "Or from Martinique or Guadalupe." The banter was just beginning—but was already going to my head like a double shot of *eau de vie.*

"Why not from French Guiana?" I said. "Or from New Caledonia?"

"Funny, you don't *look* Haitian—or Senegalese or Algerian."

“Ah, but ‘beauty is only *sin* deep,’” I said. “Saki”—I then offered together with a blush. (I was showing off, and he knew it.) Still, he seemed to be impressed with my ‘knowledges’—at least in geography and literature—and I wasn’t going to give up this hook if I could keep him hanging from it.

“That could only have come from a Frenchma—uh, woman,” he said. He pronounced ‘woman’ in a low tone somewhere between a murmur and a rumble—and I knew in that instant that he was no more gay than the man in the moon. It was, I realized, my first real experience of what we French call ‘*un coup de foudre*’—and I expected to hear a thunderclap at any instant. If not from the sky, then from my heart—or at least from my groin.

He stepped in my direction and held out his hand. “My name’s M—,” he said. But I lost everything after M— to Noa’s brief scream and a pair of audible thumps as her head hit first the bar on the way down—and then the ground.

I was dumbstruck; caught in a panic. Accidents can happen anytime, anyplace, but why did one have to happen to *me* on my first day in America? Luckily, M— was caught in no such thing. As Noa lay on the ground in a state of unconsciousness, he bent down and carefully probed for damage to her neck or spine. She was bleeding profusely from a cut on her forehead, and the sight of it made me dizzy. But M— seemed unconcerned about the blood, more anxious about her unconsciousness.

At that moment, another mother ran up to us, cell phone in hand. "Shall I call an ambulance?" she asked, the voice of rationality and action.

"Yes, please do," M— said in an equally rational and calm voice. He then looked up at me. "Where does she live?" he asked matter-of-factly.

"Right there," I said—pointing across the street. It was the only English I could conjure up under the circumstances.

M— picked Noa up carefully, then turned to the lady with the cell phone. "Please have them send the ambulance to Richardson Street, right across from the entrance to Tiffany Park. We don't know the street number, but someone will flag them down when the ambulance gets here. Okay," he then said to me, "let's go."

By the time we arrived at the house, the front of M—'s shirt was blood-soaked. Laura must've heard our arrival, as she entered from the garden as soon as we pushed open the front door. If anything registered on her face when she saw Noa's condition, I'd have to call it 'reserve.' She ushered M— over to the sofa, and then with a gesture indicated that he should lay Noa down.

"Saul?" she called. Although nothing accompanied the sound of her voice but the slightest hint of urgency, Saul responded immediately.

"What have we here?" he asked more to himself than to any of us when he shortly arrived. And then, as if looking at a Petri dish or a math equation. "Would you please bring me a wet washcloth, darling?"

While Saul probed in much the same way M— first had, and then looked satisfied that nothing other than skin had been broken, Laura went upstairs to the bathroom to retrieve a washcloth. M—, meanwhile, explained what had happened.

"Looks like your little nugget took a Vonnegut," he said to Laura when she returned a moment later and handed Saul the damp washcloth. He then began to dab the cut on Noa's forehead. "It's just a superficial wound," he said. "May require a few stitches, but it looks much worse than it is." He continued dabbing, and the blood indeed seemed to stop flowing. "I'm more concerned about her unconsciousness."

As if on cue, Noa opened her eyes—then blinked them a few times as she looked up at the four of us. "*Ow*, Mommy," Noa said as she came to. Laura immediately knelt down next to Saul.

"It's nothing, nugget. Just a little scratch."

"I took a Vonnegut," Noa said with just the hint of a pout.

"You did indeed," Saul said. "So much for your modeling career, I'm sorry to say. 'Looks like you're going to have to start gearing up for astrophysics."

"Or perhaps for anthropology," Laura said with an affectionate nudge to her husband. "I don't think it's all *that* bad."

I heard in the distance—but heading audibly in our direction—what I suspected might be the sound of an ambulance siren, although it was quite different from—somehow more strident than—our French sirens. Indeed, within seconds, it pulled up outside the entrance to the park, and M— went promptly out the front door to let the attendants know where we were.

Undoubtedly alarmed at the sight of M—'s blood-soaked shirt, one of the attendants threw open the front door and barged in. "How we doin' here, folks? Where's the victim?"

From his crouched position next to Noa, Saul answered. "More like the agent than the victim. She did it to herself."

"Daddy!" Noa said.

"Ah, my little juggernaut. As Mommy and I have told you since the instant you emerged from the womb, actions have consequences. You wanna come out? Deal!"

A second attendant came through the door carrying what looked like a truckload of emergency paraphernalia, his walkie-talkie pumping out commands as he walked. All of the commotion and strange faces unfortunately had an effect quite contrary to what Noa's parents had managed to accomplish, and she looked as if she were about to start crying.

"What's this, Mommy?" she said.

"These people are just doing their jobs, nugget. Nothing to worry about." The second attendant called in, I suppose, a report. I couldn't understand a word of what he was saying—or of what the person at the other end was answering—as most of it sounded to me to be in some kind of code.

"Would you like us to take her in, ma'am?" he asked as he turned his head to Laura.

Laura looked at Noa. "Would you like to ride in an ambulance, nugget?"

"*No,* Mommy! Why do I have to go *anywhere?"*

"We're going to have to get you fixed up again, Noa," Saul said. "I can see your brains through the hole in your head. And while the matter's not exactly grave, it *is* gray."

"What does Daddy mean, Mommy?"

"Daddy's just being silly, nugget. You're going to have to get a few stitches to close the wound on your forehead. You don't want to have a scar, do you?"

"Like the one on your belly, Mommy?"

"Exactly!"

"Yuck!"

"Well, it's not *that* ugly, is it?" Laura said, pretending to be miffed. She'd managed, once again, to put Noa at ease as she stood up to face the attendant. "We'll take her to the hospital. If you'd be kind enough to call ahead and alert the attending physician that we have a rag doll on hand who'll need a bit of mending, I'd be very grateful.

"Yes, ma'am. Will do."

"Well, there you are, nugget. We'll just put you into your car seat and take you there ourselves." She then turned to M—. "I'm sorry. I believe we neglected to introduce ourselves and thank you for all your help. I'm Laura Nelson, and this is my husband, Saul Perlmutter," she said as she extended her hand. "I assume you've already met Marie-Claire."

M—, who'd remained quietly in the background until that instant, stepped forward and extended his own hand. "A pleasure," he said. "And I'm—."

The sound of a mother's scream from across the street cut him short once again. "Oh, my God!" she screamed. "Whose little boy—?"

M— seemed suddenly to remember that he had a charge, and that he'd neglected that charge in focusing all of his attention and efforts on Noa. *"Eh, mon Dieu!"* he said as he ran to the front door.

He crossed the road and entered the park in what looked like a single leap. I followed directly behind him, though not as speedily. As soon as I got through the entrance, I saw what had happened: it was in fact the little boy he'd accompanied to the park in the first place—now also fallen from the monkey bars and lying unconscious on the ground. He wasn't bleeding, however—or at least not that I could see as I approached the scene and slipped through the small throng of mothers surrounding his motionless body.

The Emergency Medical Technicians came up behind me, excused themselves, and pushed on through. After a quick inspection of the little boy, one of them radioed back to the ambulance asking for a stretcher. M— looked worried, but stood aside and let them do their job—then climbed into the ambulance before it sped off, its siren once again blaring.

As I lumbered back to the house, a combination of despondency and nervous exhaustion reduced me, too, to a rag doll. In the space of only one day in the New World, my list of accomplishments could be summed up as: two children injured due to my neglect; a host and hostess I could at best have disappointed; and a man who'd entered my life like a comet, but whose identity had remained just as fleeting. I was not Jean d'Arc or even Marie Curie. I was simply some silly French girl whose parents thought too much of her—and whose parents' American friends would now have to adjust the record to reality.

I wanted to go upstairs and drown myself in the bathtub—at the very least, go to bed, put the pillow over my head and hope I'd die of asphyxia. A quick death would be preferable to this feeling of emptiness, worthlessness and shame.

I opened the front door and walked over to the staircase with the intention of going up to my room to consider how I might best put an end to the whole sorry mess. On the bottom stair, I saw an envelope addressed to me. It contained a note from Laura.

Dear Marie-Claire,

Please know that neither Saul nor I think you're in the least culpable for this afternoon's accident. It could've happened to any of us, and has in fact happened to me on a couple of occasions.

Make yourself at home. We'll be back shortly.

Affectionately,

Laura

P. S. Noa asked—if you're not still too tired from your long trip over from France to her house—whether you might be willing to start with the first of the *Babar* books at bedtime this evening.

If I'd ever thought I had the world's most sympathetic parents—and I did at the time, and still do today—it wouldn't have occurred to me to argue with Noa if she should one day challenge me with the same claim. I also knew that nothing like today's accident would ever have befallen Laura or Saul as a result of neglect or inattention.

When they returned home later that afternoon, Noa was wearing a bandage. She looked tired, though not too tired to reward me with a smile. *Reward?* What had *I* done to deserve her gratitude or affection? Laura and Saul also greeted me with a smile—and I made my best effort to reciprocate, weak though that effort may have been.

Laura took Noa upstairs to her bedroom, and I accompanied Saul out to the garden—where he explained to me, perhaps with just a smidgen of pride, that Noa had not so much as whimpered throughout the entire surgical procedure of nineteen stitches to her forehead. The on-duty resident had called in a plastic surgeon whose bedside manner was not only top-notch, but whose reputation as a surgeon was amply demonstrated by the skill he brought to bear on the case. In a few months' time, Noa would have no more than a memory to mark the incident.

In a matter of minutes, Laura and Noa—now in pajamas and carrying a large picture book—came back downstairs. Noa climbed up onto Saul's lap in order to give him a closer look at her book.

"*Histoire de Babar,*" Saul read just audibly enough for me to wonder yet again about his apparent command of the language.

"Babar?" Saul suddenly asked in mock surprise. "Is this book about the experiment at the Stanford Linear Accelerator Center? Looks like it. You know, the one on CP-violation in the B meson system—the difference between matter and anti-matter. Is our little lepton already starting down the road to physics?" he asked as he gave a playful pinch to Noa's cheek. "Particle physics, mind you, but physics nonetheless. I'll have to bring you in to meet Dr. Brown, our current master of particle physics in the flavor of quark."

Noa, all eyes, looked at her mother for an appropriate response.

"No, Saul. This book is about Babar the elephant. An anthropomorphized elephant, I grant you. But unlike what physicists deal with, a *true* life form."

They were bantering—just like *maman* and *papa*—but it was the banter of love—just like *maman*'s and *papa*'s love banter. I felt right at home.

Noa climbed down from her father's lap and gave me the book. "Please? Can we?"

Noa and I walked up the stairs hand in hand and entered her bedroom. She climbed in under the covers and patted the space next to her to indicate where I belonged. I propped up a pillow and sat down with my back up against her headboard, then turned to the title page. *"L'histoire de Babar, le petit éléphant," par Jean de Brunhoff.* I looked down at Noa to see whether she was following. I had the impression that if her ears could've mimicked her eyes, they, too, would now be big and round. I turned the page and continued.

"Dans la grand forêt, un petit éléphant est né. Il s'appelle Babar. Sa maman l'aime beaucoup..."

And so I continued for the first three chapters, at which point I looked down again to see that Noa was fast asleep. I slipped out of her bed and went back downstairs to the garden where Saul and Laura were sharing a bottle of wine.

Saul pulled out a chair for me to sit down on. "Would you like some?" he asked. "It *is* Californian—."

"Mercy bocoop!" I said in mock French. Saul smiled, got up from the table, went into the kitchen and brought back a wineglass. He then filled my glass to three-quarters. "Marie-Claire, would you like to come in with me to work on Monday?" he asked as he put the bottle back into an ice bucket.

"Really?" I asked.

"Really," he said. "The younger physicists there don't get out much. They're quite likely to bark or bay when they see you—or make other animal sounds to show their approval. But I think you can handle them in your own charmingly French way, right?"

"Right," I said. "Charm is my birthright. I *am*, after all, a *soupçon* of *je ne sais quoi."*

"Yes," Laura said. "As I remember, your mother was quite an abundance of the same. But *also* of intelligence."

"And both qualities would've come to you straight through the tit," Saul said.

"Saul!" Laura said. "How absolutely *boorish* of you!"

"That's me in spades. When not a boor, then a bore," Saul said with a smirk, then turned to me. "How are you with puns? Do they annoy you?"

My eyebrows arched for combat. "But neither is as bad as a boar"—two beats—"in a china closet," I said.

"Excellent!" Saul said, making a miniature show of finger-clapping. *"Superb!"* I've no doubt you'll acquit yourself well with our barbarous crew."

"Yes, Marie-Claire, I wish you much luck," Laura said. "'Barbarous' can't even begin to describe—"

"Now, darling. Your lot is any better? At least *mine* wear socks with their Timberlands."

"Very funny."

And so it is that we passed the remaining wakeful hours of the weekend. Saul and Laura sometimes caviled or quibbled, but it was only over words and definitions. I felt my English vocabulary growing in leaps and bounds—as they say—and the two of them gave me ample opportunity to expand it. English is not quite as rich in homonyms as French, but that just made my *jeux de mots* more of a personal challenge. Besides, when I got it right, Saul would congratulate me heartily—and always with the clamor of two clapping index fingers.

I didn't hear from M—, which resulted in no small chagrin. However, Noa took all of the attention I could give her during the day—while Saul and Laura gave me all of the attention *I* could possibly desire in the evening.

When Monday morning came 'round, I was ready. I didn't really know what the appropriate dress might be for a physics laboratory—and so, I decided that if I had to err, I'd err on the side of caution. I wore my best summer dress—sheer, I admit, and cut slightly above mid-thigh, but at least

I had the good sense to wear a bra. Okay, so the bra was lacy. What other kind would a French girl wear? *Ouf!*

When I walked out the front door to join Saul, he chuckled. “Marie-Claire,” he said as he put his car into gear, “I hope your presence doesn’t result in a melt-down at the lab.” I had only a vague idea of what he meant, but a girl *does* like to make a good first impression.

The Golden Gate Bridge was magnificent at that hour of the morning—though shrouded in fog or smoke or both. Saul explained that it had been a particularly dry summer and that, as a result, forest fires were breaking out everywhere. Although fog at that hour of the morning was certainly not unheard of, he suggested that what we were seeing was more likely the result of fires.

He very graciously and patiently explained what he and his team were working on so that I wouldn’t appear to be a total *ingénue.* But I had two things working for me: I was the daughter of an astrophysicist who’d spent long hours explaining the object of *his* work; and the language of physics seemed to tread a lot of common ground between the world of French and the world of English. For the first time in my life, I understood my personal debt to the Normans for their invasion.

When we arrived at the Lawrence Berkeley National Laboratory, just above the campus of the University of California at Berkeley, I felt as if I'd just driven through the Bois de Bologne in Paris—it was *that* rustic and *that* spectacular with its view of San Francisco Bay. Saul and I parked alongside the Physics Building at the entrance to which three men stood—smoking pipes and chatting—as we approached on foot.

"Ah," Saul said like the hale fellow, well met he was, "my esteemed colleagues in Dark Energy—Michael, Greg and George. Gentlemen, may I present Marie-Claire, whose last name shall remain a mystery so that none of you will be tempted to Google her image on a nudie beach in the south of France."

Only two of the men were smoking pipes at the time, and they both suddenly seemed to seize up. The third reached quickly inside his lab coat for a cigarette rather than extend a hand in greeting. Then, as if some silent signal had passed among them, all three felt it necessary to remove and wipe their glasses. I decided to take the initiative.

"Doctors, it is an enormous pleasure!" I said as I smiled and extended a hand in their general direction.

One of them abruptly looked at Saul. "And she *speaks,* too?"

"Just as long as you keep her clock wound up. She's got a little key right here," Saul said as he briefly touched the small of my back.

My hand was still extended in their general direction, but no one was taking it. I began to feel somewhat foolish until Saul once again stepped in.

"Her father is a personal friend. He does research and occasionally teaches at the Collège de France. You may've heard of it?" His question was met with blank stares. "Our own good Dr. Chu shared the N-Prize in 1997 with Bill Phillips, of the NIST, and with a gentleman of that same institution by the name of Claude Cohen-Tannoudji. Perhaps you've heard of *him?"*

Three pairs of eyes bounced back and forth between Saul and me. My smile was holding up just fine under the strain, but my arm was beginning to feel like dead weight.

"Dark energy!" the one with the cigarette whispered ominously as he looked at me—although it was plain that he was mocking himself rather than me.

"Dark *French* energy!" said another after he'd first shown me the courtesy of extracting his pipe from his mouth. *"Vive la France!"*

"Oh là là!" was all the third had to offer, as he hadn't first taken the precaution of removing his

pipe from his mouth. This little *faux pas* meant that several bits of burning tobacco were now leaping out of his pipe and onto the ground.

The Three Musketeers of Dumas had *nothing* over these stooges. '*Entre croquant; sors moquant*' had always been my motto—in birth, death, and all pit stops in between. Something like 'In with a Muse; out with amuse' in English, but I really hadn't given it much thought—and rather than think, I acted.

"Esteemed doctors of philosophy, I salute you!" I said as I grasped each one in succession by the hand and planted a quick peck on their three pairs of cheeks. "I understand that Berkeley is the new Jerusalem, and I—." What I now realized was that I had no idea where I was going with this. Luckily, Saul stepped in once again to fashion me a rescue.

"Perhaps one of you 'esteemed doctors of *philosophy*' would care to show Marie-Claire around our little skunkworks, hmm?"

It was a race to see which one would open the door first—and another race to see who could squeeze through immediately after me—with the result that all four of us became entangled as we tried to fit through the door.

I looked back briefly to signal to Saul that I'd be fine in the company of his staff—and saw him smirking in his inimitable way. It was the last I'd see of him until the end of the workday.

On the way home, we discussed my first experience at the lab, and Saul seemed to be quite amused at my narration of events as they'd occurred throughout the day... how not once had I been left alone except to visit the ladies' room—and even there, how I'd had three attentive foot soldiers standing guard just outside the door. He asked whether I had any desire to return. I thought, for at least the length of a blink, about my collection of bikinis, the beach, meditation, the horizon—and answered "Yes, *please!*" He seemed happy.

When we arrived home, no sooner had we stepped up to the front door than Noa was at it—*Babar* in hand, eyes big and round, and eyebrows huddled thick as thieves in considering how much of my time and attention she could steal. One glimpse of me told her, however, that she wouldn't have to steal a thing—that I'd happily give her whatever she could handle.

And so, for the next month, our daily routine found a comfortable path—as comfortable as any I'd ever known in my young life. And what is life (at least after adolescence) but a search for comfortable paths? On weekdays, Saul and I would go to the lab. I'd be free to assist in any way I could—whether with getting coffee and donuts for the group or with researching a question on the Internet—it really didn't matter. On some occasions, they'd actually allow me to participate in their scholarly musings and grumblings. Thanks to *papa,* my knowledge of physics was sound; thanks to my own education at the lycée, my higher math was also on solid ground; and thanks to *maman* and *papa* both, my logic sometimes outshone even theirs—okay, maybe not Saul's.

I didn't see Saul as much as I would've liked during the day—and in fact, I frequently saw his car missing from the lot whenever members of his staff and I would step out for one of their smoking sessions.

By the afternoon of my second day at 'work,' I even had my own official Lawrence Berkeley National Laboratory pocket protector. And—so that any distraction I might provide my co-workers would be more in line with pure physics—my own lab coat, over the breast pocket of which was printed 'Marie-Claire' in cursive, and on the back of which was embroidered, in big, bold letters: **Dark Lady**. I was twice blessed: in the reference to the inspiration of several of Shakespeare's sonnets, certainly, but also because I now felt I was a kind of mascot to Saul's team at Berkeley.

Evenings, as soon as we arrived home, Noa would take my hand and lead me straight up to her bedroom for another few chapters of *Babar.* Before I left at the end of August, we'd managed to cover all of both Jean and Laurent de Brunhoff's collections—and in *both* French and English.

Weekends, I'd give Laura part of the day off and spend a morning or an afternoon with Noa in one of Sausalito's several parks. I confess that my favorite remained Tiffany, and that I'd return there always in the hope that I might once again meet M—. But it was not to be. And so, Noa and I would eventually return home, and I'd retire with Saul and Laura to the garden to drink away my sorrows, just like any reasonable adult. And just like any reasonable adult, I'd keep the source of those sorrows to myself.

On my last working day at the lab, I dutifully—if also somewhat reluctantly—turned in my pocket protector and lab coat. The Dark Energy team accompanied Saul and me to the front door of the Physics Building, shook my hand, gave me French-style pecks to both cheeks followed by an American-style hug. They then resumed chatting and smoking their pipes—exactly as I'd found them the first day. As Saul and I pulled out of the parking lot, I noted how the cigarette smoker fumbled with his pack—pulling it out of his pocket, withdrawing a cigarette, putting it between his lips, then putting it back into the pack and putting the pack back into his pocket—and I understood why *papa* had perhaps not wanted to grant me this simple adult pleasure at a kitchen table in a world that now seemed to me eons distant, but which was only a month—and, soon to be, just a plane ride—away.

The next day, Laura and Saul and even Noa all got up at daybreak and accompanied me to the airport. I checked myself and my baggage in, and Saul managed to get permission for the three of them to accompany me to the gate—where, just as it had happened a month earlier in Paris with *maman* and *papa,* we chatted and waited for my boarding call. From time to time, I'd sneak a look over to see whether M— might suddenly appear, but I knew with virtual certainty my hope was in vain. Saul, I think, noticed—and sought to distract me at one point by giving me a couple of bottles of the best of his Sonoma and Napa Valley wines, also wrapped and beribboned, to take home to *maman* and *papa.* More even than in *papa*'s willingness to introduce me to a particular adult pleasure, I now discerned a larger significance in this simple exchange between my parents and my hosts: namely, that the reciprocation and sharing of something that only time, work, art and a profound respect can create goes far beyond the mere fact of an alcoholic drink.

When, half an hour later, we were called to begin boarding, Laura pulled out a bag she'd studiously kept in hiding. She first handed to Noa a small and carefully wrapped package. Noa climbed down from her seat, came to stand beside me where I was still seated and handed me the gift. I opened it and recognized the dust jacket immediately: it was an English-language version of Saint-Exupéry's *Le*

Petit Prince—something I didn't think I'd looked at in years.

I bent down to hug her, but she stopped me and made me open the book to the inside cover. There, in a child's hand, she'd written—and now recited from memory:

"*On ne voit bien qu'avec le coeur. L'essentiel est invisible pour les yeux.*"

I was dumbfounded. Not only had she memorized one of the most often-quoted lines from the story, she'd also recited it without appreciable accent. Where could this have come from? I looked at Noa in astonishment and gratitude, then let her fall in under my arm.

Laura next pulled a package out of the same bag and handed it to me—so I'd know it was from her. It was weightier and somewhat larger than Noa's gift. I opened it and found...another book—this one by Franz Boas and titled *The Mind of Primitive Man.* Noa once again reached up and opened the book to two inscriptions under two different sets of initials—though both were written by the same adult hand:

> "I hope the discussions outlined in these pages have shown that the data of anthropology teach us a greater tolerance of forms of civilization different from our own, that we should learn to look on foreign races with greater sympathy and

> with a conviction that, as all races have contributed in the past to cultural progress in one way or another, so they will be capable of advancing the interests of mankind if we are only willing to give them a fair opportunity." F. B.
>
> "*N. B.* And that includes even the French!" L. N.

I looked at Laura and could see that she was struggling to suppress a guffaw. "I'm sorry, Marie-Claire. I just couldn't resist. I hope I haven't offended you."

My ear-to-ear smile put that fear quickly to rest.

Laura then pulled out a third gift and handed it to Saul—who in turn handed it to me. It was not like the others—so, obviously not a book. I opened it and found within… my lab coat and Lawrence Berkeley National Laboratory pocket protector. It was one of those moments when I suddenly felt very small, very unprotected, very vulnerable—and I'm certain that my inability to look up from my lap provided the proof of it, if proof indeed needed to be provided. Just to tip the scales in his further favor, perhaps, Saul reached out and turned the lab coat over. His team—ostensibly nonchalant on my last day at the lab—had clearly been busy in anticipation of this moment. The revised embroidery read **Dark Energy's Dark Lady**. The reference to the source of Shakespeare's inspiration that at one time had been merely oblique was now official.

I could no more hold back the tears at that moment than I'd been able to hold them back a month earlier with *maman* and *papa* in the airport in Paris. They flowed, and now the charge apparently fell to Noa to put her arms around me and give me a comforting pat on the back.

When I was eventually able to look up and smile, Laura handed me a Kleenex—to which Saul then affixed something like a July 4th sparkler, figuratively speaking: "*Il y a un quatrième cadeau, mais il arrivera seulement lorsque tu te trouves réinstallée à Paris.*"

The announcement of a final boarding call came over the public address system, and I realized that Saul had waited until the last possible moment to make his own little announcement. It was not, however, only his mention of "another present" waiting for me in Paris that took me by surprise; it was also that he chose to deliver the message in French—with ease and without even a *soupçon* of an accent. I felt quietly betrayed, but then reflected for an instant: who had actually benefited most from my ignorance? Why, me, of course!

"*Merdre!*"

"Alfred Jarry," Saul said—and smiled cunningly. "*Tout Ubu.*"

"*Soit!*" said Noa.

"*Ça y est,*" Laura added by way of conclusion—following which we indulged in a five-second-long group hug. I then quickly gathered up my gifts and ran to present my boarding pass just before they would've closed the door on the 'caterpillar' leading from our boarding gate to the aircraft. I turned to wave one last time, and also looked one last time over their shoulders to see whether—. But my eyes were misting over again, and I could no longer focus. And so, I turned around and walked out to my plane.

Before sitting down and belting myself in, I pulled a blanket out and stored my presents and the bottles of wine in the corner of the overhead bin—all except Noa's gift, which I put down on the seat next to mine.

Half an hour later, we were climbing—and I strained to see the Golden Gate Bridge and, just beyond it, Sausalito. I put on my headphones and set my iPod to Samuel Barber's "Adagio for Strings"—sentimental perhaps, but it was the sound and mood I wanted as I left San Francisco and the New World. Besides, Samuel Barber and this particular piece had been an earlier present from Saul and Laura, together with Pachelbel's *Canon*.

I turned to the last bit of dialogue between the little prince and the fox, where I knew I'd find the English-language version of Noa's inscription:

> "Goodbye," said the fox. "And now here is my secret, a very simple secret: It is only with the heart that one can see rightly; what is essential is invisible to the eye."

I considered for a moment whether Laura or Saul would've instructed her to take this little passage as her dedication—or whether she, herself, would've discerned the simple wisdom of it. If the latter, Noa was indeed an exceptional child.

I next turned to another of my favorite passages—this one, between Saint Exupéry and the little prince:

> "All men have the stars," (the little prince) answered, "but they are not the same things for different people. For some, who are travelers, the stars are guides. For others, they are no more than little lights in the sky. For others, who are scholars, they are problems. For my businessman they are wealth. But all these stars are silent. You—and you alone—will have the stars as no one else has them—"
>
> "What are you trying to say?"

> "In one of the stars, I shall be living. In one of them, I shall be laughing. And so it will be as if all the stars were laughing, when you look at the sky at night... You—only you—will have stars that can laugh."

I thought of the people closest to me—of *maman*, the anthropologist; of *papa*, Saul and Laura, the astrophysicists; of Robert, *ouf!*, the scatologist or scatologician—certainly *one* of the two in any case; and finally of Noa. They were all, in my mind, now stars—little laughing stars. But I wondered whether I'd retain that image in just a few more hours when a dark sky over the Atlantic would greet my little window with a basketful of *real* stars. Would they already just be guides? And, if so, what would they be to me once I became an adult? Would those stars simply turn into problems to be solved—as they were for *papa*, Laura and Saul—or would I, like any ordinary businessman, see them as a source of wealth? Could one actually *act* on the wisdom of Saint Exupéry in real life and still hope to become something more than a star-gazing shepherd?

Here I'd arrived in the New World all set to conquer it—and I suppose, in a certain sense, I had. At the same time, however, it had conquered me. It had shown me that having a pretty face was certainly an advantage—but that a pretty face didn't entitle me to a monopoly on others' affections or attention. It had shown me that French charm and wit could go a long way towards winning those affections and that attention—but that neither charm nor wit alone could win true friends. It had shown me that the only way to earn and keep another's love was to invest, to work, to show respect of another's needs, wants and feelings. I thought of the dialogue from which Noa had excerpted her dedication and turned once again to that chapter:

> "It is the time you have wasted for your rose that makes your rose so important."
>
> "It is the time I have wasted for my rose—" said the little prince, so that he would be sure to remember.
>
> "Men have forgotten this truth," said the fox. "But you must not forget it. You become responsible, forever, for what you have tamed. You are responsible for your rose..."
>
> "I am responsible for my rose," the little prince repeated, so that he would be sure to remember.

I thought first of Noa, but then of M— and of what we might've been, might've become, before I turned to the first conversation between the fox and the little prince:

The fox gazed at the little prince for a long time.

"Please—tame me!" he said.

"I want to, very much," the little prince replied. "But I have not much time. I have friends to discover, and a great many things to understand."

"One only understands the things that one tames," said the fox. "Men have no more time to understand anything. They buy things all ready-made at the shops. But there is no shop anywhere where one can buy friendship, and so men have no friends any more. If you want a friend, tame me…"

"What must I do to tame you?" asked the little prince.

"You must be very patient," replied the fox. "First, you will sit down at a little distance from me—like that—in the grass. I shall look at you out of the corner of my eye, and you will say nothing. Words are the source of misunderstandings. But you will sit a little closer to me, every day…"

The next day, the little prince came back.

> "It would have been better to come back at the same hour," said the fox. "If, for example, you come at four o'clock in the afternoon, then at three o'clock I shall begin to be happy. I shall feel happier and happier as the hour advances. At four o'clock, I shall already be worrying and jumping about. I shall show you how happy I am! But if you come at just any time, I shall never know at what hour my heart is to be ready to greet you... One must observe the proper rites..."

M— and I certainly started out on the right foot, I thought. But then? Well, as *papa* had often reminded me, life's not always fair.

It was while trying to remember the details, the particulars of a face I'd seen only once and of a voice and laugh I'd heard only once—and in trying to remember the sensation of my first *coup de foudre*—that I drifted off to sleep.

Hours later, it became obvious to me that I'd slept through the night—short as it was—and then woken up only as people were beginning to lift the window-screens in preparation for breakfast. I looked out of my own window, then down—where I could see nothing but clouds. Instead, I looked at a map of the plane's itinerary posted on the video screen and saw that we were just then passing over the coast of Ireland, would shortly cross the Irish Sea, would then fly over a portion of Wales, followed by Devon, Cornwall, and finally the Channel to begin our descent over my beloved Normandy. As I looked at the horizon—something, I reminded myself with a chuckle, I'd done not even *once* from a California beach—I could see the sun just barely climbing up over the edge of the planet. It was nothing less than glorious from this vantage point, and I wondered whether pilots might ever really grow indifferent to the sight of it at dawn.

I knew from the previous day's telephone conversation with *maman* that both she and *papa* would be waiting for me at Charles de Gaulle airport in Roissy—and I considered how fortunate I was to have been born into this one family, but also to have recently become acquainted with another equally extraordinary family. It was the time each had "wasted" for me, their "rose," that made me so important to them. And, I suppose, in the view of Saul and Laura and even Noa, it was the time I had "wasted" on them—particularly on Noa—that made them and her so important to *me.*

I was seated on the port side of the aircraft this time, as I'd wanted to get one last look at the Golden Gate—but this meant I wouldn't now be seeing the *Cité* from my own window. As we continued our descent in preparation for landing, what I saw instead was the outskirts of Paris—Pontoise and Taverny—and I felt riven between the comfort on the one hand, and the ennui on the other, of the familiar. And yet, it was precisely the thought of seeing familiar faces—namely those of my own family—that now produced in me a genuine excitement.

As I came off the plane, I saw them standing, waiting … *maman, papa*, and—if I wasn't hallucinating—Robert. Had the attendant slipped something into my coffee? Robert up at this hour? For *me?*

I ran to them like a little girl—unabashed, unashamed, undisturbed and imperturbable by whatever anyone around might think when seeing a young woman of my age running into the arms of her family. It had been only thirty days—and yet, it had been thirty days far from home. I lifted my face to the three of theirs, and we engaged in some *a*typically French behavior. *Papa—mais bien sûr!*—was the first to restore Gallic order.

"*Alors, mon trésor, bienvenue chez toi.*" If *chez moi* was now Charles de Gaulle airport, I figured I was about to learn some rather disturbing news. I knew, however, what *papa* really meant—and, what was much more, I noted that for once he hadn't made a *jeu de mots* of his endearment. *Papa* eschewed puns only under the most serious circumstances, and I suspected this might be one of them.

"*Merci, papa. J'en suis ravie.*" A tad hyperbolic? Perhaps. But the entire situation invited hyperbole.

"Should we now speak only English with you?" he asked. "Have you lost your French knowledges, *mignonne*?"

"*Non, papa. Je les ai pas perdues,*" I said. "*En effet, je les ai approfondies. 'Une langue, c'est un océan dont on ne connaît que les bords,*" I reminded him. "*Et cependant, j'ai creusé pas mal de sable afin d'en relever des perles—en anglais* et *en français.*"

He smiled. "*Mon petit philologue,*" he said. "*Toi, d'intelligence avec mon petit Robert"*—at which point he placed his hand affectionately upon my little brother's shoulder—"*alors, je suis vaincu.*" It was a concession—but also a high compliment he was paying me at that moment—and he knew it. I was no longer his budding astrophysicist—and, as I looked into *maman*'s eyes, I knew that *she* also knew I wasn't bound for the same.

Once we'd retrieved my luggage, we headed out to the car. I bantered with Robert about how he'd spent four horrible weeks without me—and yet there was a newer quality to our chat. He was not the absolute *con* I'd known for the better part of three years. Instead, it seemed to me that he almost wanted to hold my hand; that he wanted to make sure I wouldn't escape again; that I wouldn't abandon them. It was endearing, to say the least.

Papa and *maman* said very little to me in the car, but that didn't exactly come as a surprise. I'd known them long enough—and knew, too, that my time would come.

And so, when we finally arrived home, I took my bags up to my room to await a summons or a visit.

As soon as I entered my room, I noticed that it looked—no doubt, thanks to *maman*—as if I'd never left it. Everything was in its place. The familiar, I now thought, has both its consolations and its comforts. I sat down on my bed just to breathe familiar air—and that's when I saw it on my pillow: a letter with a week-old postmark and a Canadian stamp. The return address was '*rue* so-and-so,' *Montréal*. The name above the return address was one I didn't recognize.

I opened the letter. It was written in French—in an elegant hand, as elegant as a voice and laugh I'd heard only once, half a world away. I quickly turned to the end of the letter—and saw the name '*Michel.*'

My heart was in my throat. *Papa* might disapprove of such an expression, but it was true. My heart *was* in my throat. Could this be M—?

I turned back to the beginning. '*Ma trop chère Marie-Claire*' it began. And although the letter was written in French, I swear I heard it—and read it—as he had once spoken to me, in a park named 'Tiffany,' in English.

> Allow me to introduce myself. My name is Michel. I am someone you met in a small park not so long ago. The park was in the town of Sausalito, in California, U.S.A. We met briefly—until an unfortunate couple of accidents cut short our courtship. We were not able to resume that courtship for a very simple reason.
>
> As you may recall, when I met you for the first and only time, I was in the company of a young boy. He was my nephew. I was visiting my sister. I don't live in Sausalito. I live in Montreal.
>
> Why—you may ask—didn't I ever come back to find you? The answer is simple: I couldn't. I spent my remaining time in Sausalito with my nephew in the hospital.
>
> His fall left him paralyzed. At this moment, he is still in that condition. Whether or not he will recover the use of his limbs is unknown. In any case, I

cannot abandon him. I hope you can understand.

Dr. Perlmutter and I have become good friends in the space of a very short time. It is from him that I have your address in Paris. He comes daily to the hospital, almost always at mid-day, to look in on my nephew and to talk with me. He tells me you are not just *any* French girl—that you are quite *extraordinaire*—and I believe him. After all, we had a brief but extraordinary courtship, you and I—*n'est-ce pas?*

I don't know that you can forgive my absence and lack of reciprocation. I felt that day a *coup de foudre* when I spoke with you, but the lightning may've struck on my side only. Perhaps, like Benjamin Franklin, you've devised a lightning rod to deflect unwanted strikes.

If not, and if you have any little desire to see me again, I would swim the ocean to find you. We Canadians—unlike the Finns—have not the *accoutrements*; but I swear to you I would do it. (Please forgive my little *jeu de mots*; I could not resist.)

I quite like and trust Dr. Perlmutter. He is an honest and straightforward man. If he tells me you are not just any French girl, I think this has significance. Dr. Perlmutter doesn't strike me as a man who deals in insignificancies.

Please let me know your disposition. Canadian winters are long and cold. I would welcome the wealth of one warm word from you to remind me of how warm a day can be—and once was—in Tiffany Park, Sausalito, California, USA.

Respectfully, Michel

I put the letter down, but quickly picked it up again and re-read it. Yes, it was written in French—a flawless French, an unpretentious French, the French of a man of action and not just of words—my little Bonaparte. Could I become his Josephine? Perhaps—but with a notable caveat: I would have no other lover but my emperor, my Bonaparte, my Michel. If this sounded insufficiently French, *soit! Maman* and *papa* had had no other lovers—I was convinced of it. Saul and Laura—notwithstanding my original musings about his mid-day absences from the lab—had had no other lovers. In their case, the clear evidence of a happy marriage was Noa. In my parents' case, I believed the clear evidence was me. Fidelity is not an accident or the product of will-power. It's a learned behavior—like so much else in life.

I took out a pen and paper and wrote to Michel, my Bonaparte, that yes, I would 'come to Italy' immediately if he wished it—that Paris and its lights held no further allure or enticement for me. That the only light of my life—now and forever more—shone in *Montréal.* And that the thought of Canadian winters was already burning in my breast with the soft glow of a Tiffany lamp.

You may now wonder… Did any of this really come to pass? I will tell you as I write all of it, forty-plus years later, that it did—and that it came to pass exactly as I've told it.

I finished up my *bac* in Paris and moved to Montreal the following summer. Michel and I enrolled at McGill University and were fortunate to find a little apartment on the Rue Redpath, right alongside the Parc Percy-Walters, where we spent the next twelve years in our separate academic pursuits.

I did not, in the end, choose a career in philology; I left that instead to Robert, who ironically followed my parents' love of words right into a prestigious editorial position with Larousse. He's still there. "*Je sème à tout vent…*" ("I sow to all winds…") "*…celles qui m'aiment constamment.*" ("those who love me too well.") he likes to say with a chuckle. At one point, he was even inducted into *l'Académie,* where he has, to this day, enjoyed all of the fruits of that august institution. I must say, however, that only Robert really knows what moves him *en son for intérieur.*

I instead chose to pursue a career in child psychology, where I've hardly lacked challenges and rewards. Michel—whose nephew never recovered from the accident and who subsequently died in his sleep on his eighteenth birthday—chose medicine: specifically, pediatric neurology. Both of us became doctors—and even occasional lecturers—but neither of us ever thought to weigh our names down with the tag of 'professor.'

We tried for many years to start a family, but weren't successful. Whether I was barren or he was sterile is something we chose not to investigate—it simply didn't matter, as we were both surrounded by others' children on a daily basis. Besides, we've always had each other, the memory of our first mutual *coup de foudre,* and little reënactments of that original *coup* on a regular basis. There are some advantages to not having one's own children constantly underfoot….

Instead, I became—in my off-hours—an occasional gardener and an occasional poet. Roses had always been a favorite of mine, particularly (thanks to Noa) following my re-acquaintance with ***Le Petit Prince***. And so, I repeatedly raised (in a garden in my newly-adopted country of short summers—namely, Canada) bed upon bed of roses every spring and summer, with some herbs and assorted flowers on the side. And in all of the time I spent tending to those roses, I had sufficient time to think and to compose—what else from a 'Dark Lady?'—Shakespearean/ Elizabethan/English sonnets.

Here, for what it's worth, is one of my most recent. As you can see, I've grown older (and perhaps wiser), but I haven't lost my love of *jeux de mots*. After all, I'm still French!

A Rose is but a Rose

I notice how my roses rush to bloom

(much like my grapes, now primed for wine and fun);

yet roses feel their petals steeped in gloom

once autumn drops a dimmer on the sun.

My roses sense a turning of the earth

away from what illumines summer skies.

A rose is but a rose upon her birth,

yet regal to the root until she dies—

though we are not. Instead, and in the act

of seeking to bedazzle with a blush,

we're forced to face one incidental fact
our dotage leaves us barely fit to flush.
Ha! Roses claim what stuns both puns and quips
is merely treacle from rosaceous hips.

What, then, became of Saul and Laura and Noa? Saul went on to win a Nobel Prize, while Laura earned other accolades in too numerous to count. Noa? Little Noa grew up to be a beautiful and happy woman—and then became an accomplished poet in her own right. They say in the New World that the first generation—those who emigrate from old Europe or from other parts of the world—work like dogs at whatever must be done for their children's education; that the second generation—the children—become doctors, lawyers, professors or professionals of one stripe or another; and that the next generation—the grandchildren—become artists. We know, of course, the lot of most artists. And so, the worm—or at least the wheel—turns.

I wonder what the Chinese would make of all of this.

And finally, what of *maman* and *papa?* They lived long and happy lives and reaped their own share of awards and recognition before they retired to our little country home in *Basse-Normandie*. They could've both been buried with honors in the

Cimetière du Père Lachaise, but they chose instead to be buried together—they actually died within days of one another—in a plot out at the end of our country garden. *Papa* insisted that he be buried with a bottle of his best bourgogne and *two* wineglasses—and told *maman* that if she didn't hurry up, he'd find another woman to drink with. Say of him what you will, *papa* remained French right up until the end.

Oh, and speaking of end—that business about the end of the world in August of 2008 when they turned on the Large Hadron Collider at CERN? Well, the end didn't happen. The strangelets stayed estranged—at least to us. Did I, personally, have a hand in preventing the catastrophe? Well, you don't think the Dark Energy team at the Lawrence Berkeley National Laboratory called me their 'Dark Lady' for nothing, do you? *Ouf!*

** The End **

Made in the USA
Monee, IL
04 March 2024

5708a12d-04c7-4722-8966-6dbe28ffe519R02